Joram Piatigorsky once again delivers on a promise made in his past work, offering both depth and astounding insight into human nature. Where his previous work focused more on love and yearning, *Notes Going Underground* takes us into much darker alleyways, those that meander through the vast shadowy landscape between life and death. While this may seem frightening, we are never on the journey alone. Rather, Piatigorsky serves as our chaperone, probing characters to their existential core with a blend of first-person narration that searches out not only what is truly at stake for the soul of each character – but for the soul of each story. The writing is elegantly conceived and reminds us that fiction can – and should – take us out of ourselves and put us squarely, directly into harm's way. A remarkable storyteller, Piatigorsky's beautifully blends the often-remote nature of dying with what he calls the 'privilege of life' – with humor, poignancy and even a certain romantic fantasy. *Notes Going Underground* is one of those books that other writers will secretly wish they wrote themselves.

— **James Mathews, author of *Last Known Position***

This extraordinary work of imagination, a series of thought experiments, literally turns death upside down, into a prism of life. In these stories ripe with complexity and character, Piatigorsky explores the borderline of relationships facing the ultimate breaking point, mixing the profound with the simple and always finding the most human element. A pleasure to read, they leave you thinking and imagining. What more can one ask from good fiction?

— **Ken Ackerman, author of *BOSS TWEED: The Corrupt Pol who Conceived the Soul of Modern New York, and YOUNG J. EDGAR: Hoover and the Red Scare, 1919-1920.***

"Dying is very relaxing," we learn in *Notes Going Underground*. One character attends his own funeral to hear unexpected praise from unforeseen sources. Another makes a mistake; he attends the wrong funeral. A third meets her father for the first time before he tries to cross the "*No Trespassing* law of Nature." "Dead and alive at the same time? That's absurd!" Joram Piatigorsky writes. Or is it? In a series of short stories, Joram creates an intriguing world between life and death. In his professional life, Joram made scientific discoveries others had not imagined. *Notes Going Underground* is a fascinating read that makes you wonder what we still have to learn about life and how it ends.

— Mark Cymrot, author of *Squeezing Silver*

Bravo…a masterful storyteller that makes me feel under a spell…the stories emerge irresistibly as gems because the thoughts and writing are so exquisite…on the cusp of greatness.

— Anthony Pitch, author of
***They Have Killed Papa Dead* and other books.**

Piatigorsky delivers a riveting book about death that's alive with brilliant prose and pathos. We'll all get there in time, but Piatigorsky illuminates the ultimate journey with special meaning.

— Neal P. Gillen, author of *Rendevous in Rockefeller*
and other books and short stories.

This intriguingly dark collection of short stories by Piatigorsky (Jellyfish Have Eyes, 2015, etc.) considers the possibility of a transitional stage between life and death. "I cannot fathom my own death," writes scientist Piatigorsky, "however, the mind and imagination can…indulge in fantasies…that challenge our concepts of death and being human." This collection of six short stories does exactly that. The first, "Notes Going Underground," is written from the perspective of a research scientist who finds he has been given a "grace period" between life and death to "size up" his life before burial. In "My Funeral," a biomedical scientist discovers that once dead, he continues to feel alive and attends his own memorial service. "Waking up Dead" continues in a similar vein with a protagonist who doesn't realize he is dead and continues his life as usual. The imagination-stretching "Death by Drowning" is about a daughter who connects with an absent father who has been jailed for misusing government funds when researching jellyfish, only for him to die in a bizarre manner. "Mr. Blok" ponders the state of dying after the protagonist falls into a ditch, and "What's Alive" takes the form of an essay examining the gray area between life and death. The writing is playfully morbid. In "Mr. Blok" an unnerving pleasure arises from the process of dying: "Lying on his back in the mud, soft and warm, with his eyes closed, in the marvelous quietness made him feel almost grateful and glad. How amazingly simple it is to be dead." Piatigorsky's prose is laconic yet elegant—always keen to confront the reader with probing questions: "Is a virus dead? Is the peeling bark of a eucalyptus tree alive?" The result is a deeply thought-provoking collection that presents an unflinching examination of a taboo subject. The first three offerings read as a reworking of the same story, each about a scientist negotiating the partition between life and death. Still, despite blurring into one another, these stories capture various aspects of the same phenomena. Accompanied by suitably macabre illustrations by Carrillo, this book is an intriguing read. Penetrating, inventive writing that challenges perceptions of what lies beyond the veil.

— ***Kirkus Reviews***

NOTES GOING UNDERGROUND

Notes Going Underground

Stories

by

JORAM PIATIGORSKY

Adelaide Books
New York / Lisbon
2020

NOTES GOING UNDERGROUND
Stories
By Joram Piatigorsky

Copyright © by Joram Piatigorsky

Cover design and illustrations by Ismael Carrillo
Artwork on page 7 by Lona Piatigorsky

Author photo by Margaret Dimond

Published by Adelaide Books, New York / Lisbon
adelaidebooks.org

Editor-in-Chief
Stevan V. Nikolic

All rights reserved. No part of this book may be reproduced in any manner whatsoever without written permission from the author except in the case of brief quotations embodied in critical articles and reviews.

For any information, please address Adelaide Books
at info@adelaidebooks.org

or write to:

Adelaide Books
244 Fifth Ave. Suite D27
New York, NY, 10001

ISBN: 978-1-951214-52-4

Printed in the United States of America

To Sivan, Dalia, Klara, Reuben and Tobias, my wonderful grandchildren and the wave of the future.

Lona Piatigorsky

Contents

Preface

We are imprisoned by two inescapable facts – death and being human. Death, ironically life's signature, kills without compassion or distinction between royalty and commoner, or young and old, or rich and poor. Death seals our ultimate fate that can neither be negotiated nor evaded. Our genes are the other prison sentence. As a leopard cannot change its spots, a human cannot become a different animal or sense the environment as any other species. We see the world through a human lens, with its benefits and limitations.

I accept that my senses will be confined to those of humans, and that my body will cross the sharp boundary between life and death on Earth when the time arrives.

Yet, despite full knowledge and acceptance of our restricted life, I cannot fathom my own death. My Last Will and Testament feels like a work of fiction and does not eradicate imaginary roots that anchor me in life forever. I know I'll die someday, but I still feel immortal and cannot imagine not existing. Also, I cannot even imagine how a cat or snake or fish or any other animal, even a primate, views life or death.

However, the mind and imagination can wander into foreign territories and indulge in fantasies with different rules that challenge our concepts of death and being human. The following tales explore a porous, overlapping border, both real and imagined, between life and death, and between humans and other species. Never mind crossing the boundaries of today's reality or common experiences. Free your imagination and let it breathe; there may come a time when such fantasies trespass our accepted borders and revise past experiences and future expectations.

Notes Going Underground

Ladies and gentlemen, thank you for inviting me – an ordinary man who, like most, thinks himself special but knows he isn't – to deliver my own eulogy at my funeral. It has taken much soul searching whether or not to accept your invitation. I asked myself, why should I, or anyone, deliver a eulogy at my funeral? Why not just say, "Good-bye," and let it go at that? Does a life need an explanation? I still am who I was. Dying hasn't changed my status or anything else. I had nothing to do with my birth, so I can't explain that. I came and now I'm leaving, just like any squirrel in the garden that was born and dies. There's always another squirrel. Anyway, who would believe a eulogy to myself? Praise would be taken as self-promotion and belittling myself would be considered false modesty. Isn't that what you thought when I called myself an ordinary man?

Death has always been considered an abrupt process, like crossing a line from living flesh to dead meat. A person was either alive or dead, never both at the same time, like I am now. Due to modern technology, the final stages of death can be digitized and captured in slow motion. This lets me talk to you during a suspended state of being partially alive and partially dead simultaneously, as my remaining life leaks into my corpse in the lovely coffin by my side. This gives me a grace period while still breathing to reminisce – size up my life – in preparation for burial. It's not physically painful and I don't like it, but it is what it is: we're born slowly and die slowly. We have tapered ends, so to speak. Only when my entire life has passed – in today's lingo, has downloaded – into my corpse will I fade out and go underground.

I first was exposed to gradual death at college in a physiology course when I decapitated a turtle to study its heart. Not only did the heart continue beating for hours, but the headless body of the turtle continued walking for some time! It made me wonder whether the bodiless head was still seeing or thinking for a while, or whatever turtles did with their brains, and if so, for how long?

What a disturbing notion: a guillotined head still thinking in a basket!

I asked a friend for advice on what I might say at my eulogy. "Tell them about a few of your career contributions and recognitions, and the love and support you received from family and friends, like me," he advised. Then he suggested some nonsense that I talk about being a down-to-earth regular guy who roots for the local sports teams and likes to eat desserts before entrees. I have an incurable sweet tooth. He also added a stupid joke that I can't even remember. I guess he thought I should appear like a successful mensch, everybody's good guy. But, is that really me? A mensch who tried his best? That seems as lame as describing me as "nice." Yuk! Why not include that I rescued a puppy from the pound once?

Getting to the essence of a human being – of me in this case – giving a eulogy that's honest and worthwhile – is impossible due to the many contradictions, inconsistencies and conflicts in anyone's life. Moreover, we all, including me, have suppressed ghosts begging to get out of our skin, playing havoc with our psyches, and like it or not, are silent partners of our complex identity. I've pondered at length to understand who defines my identity: me or others ("us" or "them")? It's both, I think, which creates a conundrum. If I give my own eulogy, how others perceive me – my "them" identity – will be absent; if someone else gives my eulogy, my view – my "us" identity – will be lost.

So, here's my plan, even if imperfect. I will tell a story, a true story involving several sides of myself (cryptic perhaps), and let you draw your own conclusions. Keep in mind that we're more than one person, and you'll appreciate how slippery identity is and how incomplete eulogies really are.

A man of middle age and medium height, an average looking man, a life-long bachelor, was walking down the street in tattered clothes and a light green jacket in Chicago on a gray afternoon in January. The wind chill was in the teens and piles of dirty snow lined the street. This gentleman – and I call him a gentleman because of his gender, not style – lived in a poorly furnished, one room apartment in a shabby section of town. His prized possession was a rust-colored ceramic vase, the only present he ever received from his alcoholic father. A broken piece resulting from an accident had been glued back carelessly on the vase in its original position. He had lost track of both of his divorced parents. He supported himself by doing odd jobs and holding temporary positions from which he was usually fired because of his inability to be punctual. He was a sorrowful case. This drab January was a low point because one of his employers who occasionally paid him to take the trash to the dump had just died.

As he was ambling down the street feeling sorry for himself his eyes struck gold! The corner of what appeared to be genuine U.S. currency was protruding from a small mound of icy snow surrounding a lamppost. He leaned over and pulled it out. Yes! $20! Christmas was over for the rest of the world, but it had just started for him. He rubbed the bill with his thumb and index finger as if to assure it was real, put it in his pocket, skipped a step or two, took it out and used it to wipe his forehead, a gesture that gave it a pleasurable physical presence. He had suddenly transformed into a larger, more important person, a man with sharp eyes able to grasp opportunity and who could now afford a cup of hot chocolate with a doughnut and have change left over.

I know I'm rambling a bit, but I have always tended to drag things out. It's who I am, and it's not easy to give one's own eulogy.

Where was I?

Oh, yes, this pitiful, lonely person was cold and hungry, yet on top of the world; he had just changed from a pauper to a man with $20 in his pocket.

As he strolled, he noticed shops that he had previously ignored. A shiny $35 Timex wristwatch in a display window caught his attention. Well, that was for a king, not for him, but perhaps someday...who knows? If he could find $20, he might find $100 another time. He started kicking the snow heaps hoping that more money would tumble out.

What an optimist, driven by pipedreams.

But there was a problem. Alone the idea that $20 could grow to a larger sum made it feel lighter in his pocket. It suddenly became less money, and he was less happy. Apparently $20 was not even enough to keep track of time; that cost $35.

Poor man. He allowed a little success to balloon into greed.

The city streetlights clicked on as dusk descended. Darts of frigid air pierced his exposed face with each gust. He pulled his jacket tight around his neck and slid his frozen chest deeper into the garment when he heard a low-grade shuffling sound behind him. He turned and saw a man perilously thin – eyes bland, oversized ragged pants held up with a tattered rope, and filthy, bare toes protruding through holes in his shoes.

"Gotta dime?" croaked this pathetic bag of bones as he extended a frail arm with palm upturned.

Our newly-rich gentleman stared at the miserable excuse for a man.

"Gotta dime, even a nickel?" the beggar repeated.

"I have no loose change," came the honest response. Despite his defects, he was impeccably honest.

Our gentleman with $20, now looking like a success story by comparison, noticed that the beggar's blue fingertips trembled, and that his ring finger was a useless amputated stub. The beggar produced a phlegm-rattling cough, and pink saliva dribbled from the corners of his mouth.

Now, here's the interesting part. Our hero, if that's what he could be called, reached into his pocket, pulled out the $20, kissed it and placed it into the beggar's outstretched hand.

"God bless you," said the beggar, without looking at the amount, and he proceeded slowly down the street crunching the $20 bill in his hand.

Was this a noble act of charity? No. I knew the gentleman from high school. His name was Tim. Even as a teenager, Tim was always his own worst enemy. I remember when he ran for senior class president, craving the prestige, the power and the satisfaction of winning. What did he do? He voted for his opponent, and not because she was pretty or that he thought she was more qualified than he was. He felt voting for himself was self-indulgent, impolite, improper. He wanted it too much. Talk of a loser. That Tim gave away his $20 was entirely consistent for him.

By the way, he lost the election, by one vote!

I ran into Tim once not long ago when I was at a scientific conference in Chicago. I had gone for a walk, got lost and entered a cheap diner to ask directions. There he was, sitting with some cruddy-looking guy. Imagine the scene. Two lowly flops in a godforsaken dump having afternoon tea. One was destitute, no doubt a homeless, pathetic man who seemed too far gone to know that he was in such bad shape. The other, Tim, was struggling to stay afloat, no steady job, no family ties, no ambitions. The best thing one could say of Tim was that he didn't smell too bad. *That* one certainly couldn't say about the other guy.

It had been years since I had last seen Tim and so I focused on him, trying to remember exactly what he looked like in high school to make sure I was correct, that he was in fact Tim. The two men seemed oblivious to their surroundings and neither noticed me. Tim was doing all the talking, and the other guy occasionally responded with "uh-hum," or "yep," or "suren'uff."

In the middle of a sentence, Tim turned his head in my direction and barked, "Whadaya starin' at, buddy?"

I stammered, "Err, nothing…sorry, I mean…Tim…is that you?"

"Howd'ya know my name?" He looked startled.

"Yes, you are Tim, aren't you?" I said, amazed that I had remembered correctly.

"Yeah. Who are you?"

After I told him that I recognized him from high school, he just gazed at me with his mouth gaping, advertising his brownish, crooked teeth, and didn't say a word. That's when I discovered how long a minute can be.

Tim blanched, developed a nervous tic in his right eyelid, which kept fluttering. He ran his fingers through his greasy hair and said, "My god, it's true. Yes, I recognize you. You're just a little more wrinkled and pudgier."

I didn't mind the wrinkles, but pudgier was another matter.

Tim's voice changed, became deeper, more self-conscious, the vernacular disappeared, his eyes darted here, there, everywhere. He avoided looking directly at me.

"I'm so ashamed," he said.

I didn't know how to answer, so I reached out and touched him on the shoulder. His head tilted a notch towards my hand, his face relaxed, as if a great battle was over.

"Reckon I'll be movin' on," said the other guy. He got up and left without another word.

An indifferent waiter drying beer mugs stood behind the seedy looking counter lined with empty stools fixed to the stained wooden floor. There were no pictures on the walls, no tablecloths, no flowers or decorations of any kind. The olive-green paint was peeling off the walls, which had numerous gashes. Floor lamps standing in the corners on either side of the front door accounted for the dim light. There were no windows and the stale air had an odor of burning grease.

It was a closed environment, secluded in its own way, as was a posh country club. You were a member or an outcast. Yet, I thought, even in this dismal scene lacking charm or purpose or any class whatsoever, Tim, downtrodden and pathetic, was as human and vulnerable as I or the King of England.

After a moment of silence, Tim put his arms around my neck, rested his head on my shoulder, and cried. I felt him tremble, and his grip tightened. The waiter looked at us with a peculiar expression and went into the kitchen, leaving us alone in this miserable, stinking hole.

Tim kept repeating over and over again, "It's *not* my fault, it's not *my* fault, it's not my *fault*."

Tim had said he was ashamed, and he was, I'm sure, but it was I who should have been ashamed.

Why should I have been ashamed?

Well, unfortunate, defeated Tim, a friend from high school, most certainly a good man in need of comforting, was crying on my shoulder, begging for sympathy and un-derstanding, and what did I do? Nothing. What was going through my mind? I'm almost too ashamed to say, but, what the heck, I sense the download is nearing the end, so it's my last chance to confess. Fact is fact, and it's no different than a stone in the ground. I was thinking that Tim was dribbling snot on my new Alpaca wool sweater.

"Now, now, Tim, it's okay, really. We all have hard times now and then."

We don't all have hard times anything like that. I never did. What do I know? What right did I have to empathize? It may have been true in general, but it was dishonest coming from me. If anything, I blamed Tim for being such a loser.

"It's good to see you again, Tim," I said, another falsehood. I was thinking, "How can I get out of this?"

Just as suddenly as Tim broke down, he released his stronghold around my neck (he should have been a wrestler) and said, "Hey buddy, let's have a cup of something hot and catch up."

"S…ure," I answered, but I wanted out.

We ordered coffee (I paid) and I briefly recapped my life – research scientist, married, a couple of kids, grandkids. I was sketchy. I didn't want him to feel bad, which was presumptuous because, apart from his appearance, I had no idea what his life had been like and, anyway, I was no hero.

Then I lied again, well, I distorted the truth is more like it. I told him that I did research on hearing in earthworms, which I never had done. I worked on eyes.

"Hearing in earthworms? Do they hear?" he asked, suddenly displaying curiosity.

"Maybe,' I answered. "I'm trying to figure that out. Who knows? If earthworms can hear, at least in an earthworm kind of way, my work may help deaf people someday. Big industry, deafness."

Why did I say that nonsense and fantasy and imply that I cared about industry, which I didn't? I had modified my image to appear differently than I am. Since I didn't know much about ears or earthworms or industry, I knew I wouldn't be able to say much (I tend to talk too much), and then I could get back to the hotel sooner. I wanted to see a basketball game on TV and work on my lecture for the meeting the next day.

Tim told me of his drab life, the disappearance of his parents, how his one and only girlfriend left him, how he had dropped out of community college, how he'd given away his $20, and so on. I was hardly listening and wondering how to get out of there. Finally, I told him that I had another appointment, still another lie. He sagged a bit, like a worn drape. I felt guilty not to spend more time with him, or maybe even take him to dinner. I was selfish.

"Will we get a chance to see each other again?" he asked.

That simple question has haunted me all these years.

"Will we see each other again?" he repeated, looking earnest.

So simple, so sad, so lonely. Tim gave away his prized $20 to a miserable beggar, and I lied to have some more time to myself.

"Sure," I said. "Let's keep in touch."

He gave me his phone number, but never asked for mine. I called him once a few months later and received a recorded message that his telephone was temporarily disconnected. Temporarily, that's important; yet, I never called again. I did think about him from time to time, even worried about him, as I did about other people and causes I neglected. I collected lists of things I never accomplished, humongous lists of lost opportunities, too focused on myself to follow up. I collected absences and lived in my own head. And now, it's too late to make amends...

Wait! Why should I apologize for what I didn't do? What I did do made sense from my perspective – that's another eulogy – so apologizing for past behavior would be denying who I was. That doesn't work. I was who I was.

Did I say another eulogy? Isn't that what I implied earlier? There's never one eulogy or one story or one interpretation. There's "us" and "them". We are many people wrapped together, and we are even present in part in other people. I trust you to understand the eulogy I chose to tell, the story I told, the person, or persons, I am, in part, and was, sometimes.

Excuse me, I must sit down. My back hurts, my legs ache, my feet are numb. I'm tired, very, very tired. This must be the end…yes, it's getting darker…the lid is closing…I'm sure you can't hear me anymore…soon I'll be underground, with my notes and everything I learned along the way.

There's always another squirrel.

Published in the literary magazine *Adelaide* (December, 2018)

My Funeral

Until I experienced death, I didn't appreciate the privilege of life. Laura, my wife of 25 years, says one should live like there is no tomorrow; enjoy it, life is fleeting, there's nothing like it. I'm so sorry she had to put up with me, a curmudgeon – always complaining. But it's different now, now that I have tasted death.

Less than a year ago I didn't think that misery could enhance life. I never understood the benefit of traumatic experiences. I've changed my mind. That's what dying did for me.

It was Saturday afternoon with fantastic autumn colors. Laura, alone at home, was waiting for me, a biomedical scientist, to return for dinner after a few hours at my laboratory. A workaholic, I was trapped as usual in the paradox of trying to discover questions. I was struggling to write the final paragraph of a scientific article. Exactly how I felt at the time has faded now, like the intense green of summer leaves in the fall, but I do remember my mind straining with the words, "not good enough, not good enough." As a biomedical scientist, my work was my identity, as important to me as my life. I was merciless towards myself. Not working was not living. Surprisingly, then, dying was a relief.

My death began when I tried to stand up after an afternoon's work and suddenly my legs became lifeless pillars – dead wood. I had never felt anything even slightly like that before. I pressed the palms of my hands against the desk and pushed down, doing everything in my power to stand up. The only movement I felt was the crunching of my abs, as my personal trainer calls the stomach muscles that hide somewhere under a cozy layer of digested French fries and other delicacies.

At first, I sort of smiled. Oops, I thought, I've been sitting too long. My legs must be asleep. But oops turned to, *WHOA*, what's going on? Can you blame me for expecting my legs to respond normally, like they always did? But they didn't. It's just that simple. And then came that frightening moment: reality drifted in, and panic danced inside me.

I dialed 911 on my cell phone and pleaded, "Help me. I can't move. I can't get up. Please! Send an ambulance, quickly!"

"One moment please. I have another call. Don't go away."

Don't go away? Was he kidding? Was I delirious? I couldn't move my legs, I couldn't stand up, and my savior told me to stick around. I looked for the humor in this, but it was drowned in the sweat of anxiety. I couldn't move my legs, for Chrissake!

He returned. "Sir, are you still there?"

"What do you think?" I asked. "I can't move my legs."

"Can you breathe all right?" asked the wizard. "Do you have chest pains?"

"Let me repeat, I can't move my legs. My heart still beats. I'm at work, at my desk, I want to go home, BUT I CAN'T MOVE MY LEGS! They're lifeless. I'm scared. Please send help." I gave my address and hung up. I remember being glued to my chair and wanting to call Laura, but I didn't want to scare her. It was hard enough to deal with myself. I passed out at some point before the ambulance arrived and don't remember anything after that, so what follows is hearsay.

When the ambulance delivered me to the hospital, the receptionist got my name and address from my driver's license and called Laura. What a shock it must have been for her when she was told to come quickly, that her husband was lying like a sack of potatoes in the hospital.

They ran batteries of tests on me. The clinical diagnosis was a stroke, although both a CAT scan and MRI were normal. The doctors insisted that sometimes the causes of a stroke are very subtle, medical science is imperfect. They settled for a clinical diagnosis as the most reasonable explanation — a medical "Occam's razor" avoiding unnecessary assumptions to explain the mysterious phenomenon.

Ridiculous and dishonest! What's wrong with admitting ignorance and leaving it at that?

In any case, I was hooked up with intravenous life support, no doubt to the horror of the insurance company. They paid in full, thank goodness. Laura said she sat by me every day and held my hand. She said my fingers did not have that cold, leathery feel of death, and even twitched occasionally, reassuring her I was still alive.

I was in this suspended state of hibernation for almost four months.

Finally, I woke up, or at least I thought so.

"Bill? Oh, my god, you're moving! Can you hear me? Bill? Nurse! Come quick. I think he's waking up."

I could hear Laura's excitement and remember her precise words, although faint, as if echoing in a tunnel.

The nurse placed two bony fingers on my wrist and exclaimed in a shrill, metallic voice, "65, way higher than before. Something's happening. I'll get Dr. Riley right away." And off she went, her rapid footsteps rattling my mind. A thick silence followed the authoritative slam of the door.

When my eyes opened, I saw blurry shapes and ripples of space. Perhaps it was a dream, since I had never seen anything like this before. I had no reference point with which to compare it. Laura was sitting on the bed and I could feel her thigh against mine through the thin blanket. Her face appeared distorted, with a needle-sharp chin, and she had puffy cheeks and a flat, oversized forehead, unlike Laura's well-proportioned chin and high cheekbones covered with smooth skin. Her eyes, dark and intense, emitted hot darts into my brain that were almost painful. I remember that well, the pain.

I also noticed she was wearing her favorite blue sweater. Her chestnut-colored hair, wavy as always, swayed like seaweed in my mind. My fingers curled around her moist, trembling hand. Or was it my hand that trembled?

I remember her saying, "Bill, you're back. I can't believe it. Can you hear me?" And then she kissed me and cried.

I was conscious, but too numb to cry or show any emotion.

I stayed in the hospital for another month. There was no trace of my former paralysis. The doctors were puzzled at my recovery, but I'm convinced they didn't know what happened to me in the first place. Laura was more doting than ever. My daughter Sally and son Allen came to visit me regularly and acted as if nothing had happened. They went about their busy lives. But all was not as it seemed. How can I explain it?

My arm felt detached, as if it didn't belong to me. When I conversed, I heard the words, answered and nodded, but generally I was faking it. I didn't understand most of what I heard. My brain was scrambled. I felt immersed in a heavy fog, disoriented and alone. I was a spectator in a foreign land. That was my state for some time as I recuperated. I don't know exactly for how long. Time had little meaning for me then.

The view from the window of my hospital room, a parking lot, cars, a few trees, looked like a third-rate painting framed by the windowsill. The gray walls were the color of my existence. I was like a character in a novel written by an author who left his heart behind when his fingers struck the keyboard. I was living in the third person. I ate and slept, but my life was mechanical. I sensed that Laura knew this, but she never said anything, at least not to me. She must be a saint.

When I went home a purple banner with bright gold letters greeted me at the front door with 'Welcome Home, Dad! We LOVE you!' Laura, Sally and Allen each signed their name in a different color; Laura a bold green, Sally pink, her favorite color, and Allen black, typical for him, a confirmed pessimist. The occasion was a homemade color catastrophe that was all tenderness. As touched as I was, I actually missed the protective gray of the hospital. I remember thinking, "What's there to love? What have I done but give everyone grief?"

I wasn't the person I used to be.

A sweet aroma from flowers placed thoughtfully in the living room saturated the air, and delicious M&M's filled small bowls. Laura didn't even like the crunchy, chocolate M&M's I usually bought as a self-indulgent treat when I went away on business trips.

"Sweets for the sweet," she said. "You come first today."

"Thank you," I replied, confused why I was fighting tears of sadness. Why? I was home, able to walk, with my family who loved me.

My dog Bingo, an affectionate golden retriever and beloved family member, was my first messenger of death. Bingo was always there for me, always forgiving, bringing good cheer. He greeted me when I came home from the hospital, but not like before. He came up to me and wagged his tail, but he was sniffing with curiosity, not joy and remembrance, and then, ever so slightly, he recoiled, as if I was a stranger. He didn't rub against my leg asking for a pat on the head, a little attention, as he did with Laura and the kids. He didn't seem to know me: the person who had trained him, taught him to retrieve tennis balls, and comforted him when he shuddered with fear in thunderstorms.

We locked eyes several feet apart, his soft brown, mine blue with gray specks and hard edges. I had the impression that he was looking through me, not at me. Suddenly I was reminded of my high school days when I suffered from puppy love for my classmate Karen, who was one notch higher than perfection in my eyes. And then one day I saw her glance in that certain self-conscious way at Roy, who was taller than I was, on the football team, and had blond curls touching the upper ridges of his ears. Karen didn't even move her head, just her eyes, and then she brushed a strand of hair away from her eye with a nervous, quick motion of her hand. One silent instant, a glance, and I understood what no words could convey with the same impact.

In Bingo's eyes, I was there, but at the same time I was not there. My family did not perceive the nothingness surrounding me, but dogs are more sensitive. They hear what we don't, they smell what we can't, and they sense what we feel. My journey took another step into the unknown; I began to question my presence.

I smiled at Laura and hid my confusion.

"Good dog," I said to Bingo as he strolled out of the room.

The phone rang and Sally sprinted to get it. "Hello. Oh... hi." Her tone dropped a decibel. "I'll get him. Allen, it's Roberta," she said sullenly, handing over the receiver. I wanted to let Sally know that I understood her disappointment, to reassure her that the call she wanted, whoever he was, would come later, but instead I reached for an M&M.

I thought that the transparent shield between the world and me would disappear when I returned to work at the laboratory the next day. Everyone greeted me, but not especially enthusiastically. Too much time had elapsed, I guessed. My shell closed tighter, and the mist grew thicker. When I checked my email, I was surprised not to see the usual barrage of unwanted messages dispensing trivia, advertising products, or requesting something for me to do or send. I remembered the difficulty of catching up with these unsolicited emails even after one or two days away from the laboratory. It used to tax my patience. But now, the computer screen was empty.

I was an electronic nonentity.

I asked my assistant, Samantha, what was going on, where were my messages?

"We took care of that, Dr. Levinson," she answered blandly. "I had everything diverted to Dr. Willowby."

The phone rang and I grabbed the receiver.

It was unsettling to hear, "Dr. Willowby, please." Had Dr. Willowby taken over my office too?

"This is Dr. Levinson, William Levinson. Can I help you?" I responded.

"Who?"

"Dr. *Levinson*," I said emphatically. I was angry, which was a good feeling. At least it had passion.

"I'm sorry. I must have the wrong number." He hung up before I could explain.

When the phone rang again, I picked it up and without discussion transferred the caller to Dr. Willowby's office.

Am I really here? I wondered. The place was a beehive of activity outside the transparent envelope surrounding me. I went home early.

Laura was understanding and tried to reassure me that it takes time to get back to the old routine. "Have patience," she said. But even Laura, sweet Laura, seemed to lack conviction. She was busy with her duties as a librarian for the county, and she had made new friends during my absence whom I had never met.

I missed her, and Bingo too.

I plodded along at work for the next few weeks trying to regain contact. I even went to the office on weekends at times to read and try writing again. I attended lectures and did my best to respond to my bureaucratic responsibilities, which remained pitifully few. I was a sailboat on a becalmed sea. And then, out of thin air, I heard a voice in my mind that sounded like a trumpet announcing something important. It jolted me.

The King is dead! The King is dead! Long live the King!

The more things change, the more they stay the same. The inevitable cycle and continuity of life is universal: from the dying leaves in the fall to the birth of fresh leaves in the spring; from the breakup of a love affair to new a new lover around the corner; from disappointment to satisfaction to disappoint-ment; from high tide to low tide to high tide again. I knew that I tended to exaggerate, to interpret small signs beyond reasonable explanations. Laura would get frustrated with my melodramatic thoughts and mood swings. However, this time felt different. It occurred to me that in contrast to overreacting, I didn't stretch the possibilities enough. I was too conventional, too timid. I needed to face stark reality, to be bold.

Again, the epiphany.

The King is dead! Long live the King!

Dead-alive; alive-dead. Are these states really so different? Is a virus dead? Is the peeling bark of a eucalyptus tree alive? Is the fictional Sherlock Holmes less vibrant than his author, Sir Arthur Conan Doyle?

The blur of my daily existence snapped temporarily into focus as the fog thinned. *I was dead!* Yes. It made sense, yet it didn't. It was like the realignment of a dislocated joint. I was no longer a stranger in my isolated world. I was at home among the dead and only a visitor of no importance among the living. Dead people receive no attention.

Although the cycle of my life had not completed the circle yet – from birth to death – I couldn't stop it or run it back-wards. If I *was* dead, it would have to be a different "me" to come back again. Not me, Bill, the person I know.

The pressure was off. Stress disappeared. Relationships were abstract. The living didn't need me, nor I them. I started wondering who else around me was also dead. Surely, I was not the only one. What a limited view of death the living had.

The King is dead! Poor King. Poor me. *Long live the King!* Lucky new King. Who will it be? Dr. Willowby?

Ice, water, steam, all the same, but also different. My icy chill melted. I must be liquid now. Soon I would evaporate, my final stage of liberation. How would that happen? Would I boil and suffer small explosions? Would it hurt? Would I still be a visitor among the living, or was that temporary? Would Bingo sniff at me anymore? Would I be able to venture beyond my invisible shield? Would I still be able to think after evaporating into a gas, if that were my fate, in the great beyond? How long does it all take? What does time even mean in my transitory state?

I knew so little!

The most painful part of death for me was the loneliness. I felt neglected, even by Laura and the kids. I wasn't present. But if that were true, where was I? Everything I saw seemed like mirages without any accents of color. All sounds came from far away, somehow around the corner. Sally's soft voice was especially distant. I seldom understood what she said, but I stopped saying, "What?" It became tiresome.

Tiresome, yes. And being tired was a serious problem. I struggled not to doze off, even standing up. Every movement, walking in particular, was an effort and performed painfully slowly. Running was out of the question. The few lectures I attended at work were difficult to follow, not only due to fatigue, but also because I felt unable to understand much of what was said. Part of the problem was the hearing difficulty. But that wasn't the whole problem. I questioned my intellectual or mental abilities, which were fading. Oh, god! That loss was devastating. Life for me was working, striving to do better, having accomplishments. It was one thing to be tired or less responsive to my environment, but to lose the ability to work… that was… deadly.

It was all so confusing. My earlier anguish had involved dead legs attached to a vital body and active mind. I now had a dull mind draining life. Was I becoming demented, or was I dying slowly, in transition from alive to dead?

I felt between being a living person and an inert sculpture.

I figured that becoming fully dead was a waiting game. One foot moved ahead of the other, but I stayed in place. It was different from treading water, because I made no effort to stay afloat. I didn't need to. I was the body and the water.

One Sunday morning skimming the newspaper my eyes drifted to a short but alarming obituary. I read the headline twice to be sure I had read it correctly. It's ironic that being dead made me cautious:

Willam J. Levinson, Scientist, Dead at 53

I couldn't believe it. For the first time since my supposed stroke, or whatever ultimately killed me, I was excited. The announcement! Finally. Perhaps now I was sufficiently dead to be recognized as such. The absurdity of my death requiring confirmation from the living didn't even occur to me at the time. I had been waiting for this announcement and now it had come. It was a shock, of course, but I didn't need to pretend anymore. I was also curious about progressing to the next stage of death, presumably the final stage, which I hoped was more interesting than the bland nothingness – the loneliness – I had endured.

I was upset how concise my obituary was, no more than a mere statement of a few facts – my name, age and occupation as a research scientist. It didn't even give the names of my wife and children. Hadn't I ever done anything worth mentioning in my life? My obituary was as dry as the desert in a drought and confirmed my worst fear when I was alive: that I was not 'good enough'.

So what? Why was I still worried about my status as a living person? I no longer cared about politics and world affairs, but I was still trapped in my insecurities. It didn't make sense and frankly, it annoyed me. I was dead but not free.

I wondered how my family and colleagues would react when they read my obituary, or did they know that I was dead already? Was I noticed at all since I came out of my coma, or did I only imagine my presence? If I wasn't really there, it would explain my foggy state and constant feeling of isolation. It might also explain why the phone calls to my office were for Dr. Willowby. Maybe I just thought that I was in my office, but it was really Dr. Willowby's all that time.

All my life I believed that a person was either alive or dead. I presumed death occurred by crossing a thin line of some sort, and then, once dead, you're out of the picture, gone. I never imagined that one could feel alive and be a little bit dead – on the way to being dead, in transition, as it were – at the same time.

In any case, the obituary announced a memorial service for me on Tuesday, April 10, at 11:00 at Beth El Congregation. I hoped that my funeral would clarify things, and I looked forward to it, as weird as that sounds. Also, I was curious as to what people would say about me.

The two days before my funeral were uneventful. I felt foggier than ever trying to adjust to my official death. Neither Laura, nor my kids nor anyone at work mentioned anything about my obituary, and I didn't bring it up. I didn't even know if anyone had read it.

Death was completely different from what I expected. Frankly, I was getting sick of it.

I arrived half an hour early for my memorial service in order to get a good seat. I knew a lot of people in my life and I hoped that a number of them would appear. Of course, my parents wouldn't be there since they had passed away some time ago. My few distant relatives lived across the country, so I had to rely on my immediate family, friends and colleagues to attend my funeral.

The fact that I was still by myself in the auditorium 15 minutes before kickoff worried me. What was going on? Where was everyone? Finally, an undersized, actually tiny, middle-aged man wearing a yarmulke and a blue suit adorned with a deadly conservative blue-black tie came into the room and went to the podium, checking on things. I gathered that he was the rabbi. I had never seen him before. He nodded and said a quiet hello, very solemn-like, fairly unnerving. I began to consider the possibility that someone was playing a trick on me, but it seemed too far-fetched. I waited.

Eventually a trickle of people came into the room. But where were Laura and Sally and Allen? Where were my closest colleagues from work? Where was Timmy, my neighbor and sports-watching companion, or our friends and fellow weekend movie-goers, the Boulangers?

By five minutes after 11 there were sixteen people there, all strangers. A short, plump woman in a boring black suit was crying in the front row. She was accompanied by a somber teenage boy and a very pretty young woman in her early twenties, clearly the woman's children. I was struck by the daughter, with her cream-colored complexion and sexy figure. She did not look as distraught as her mother and brother. I must admit that I was pleased to be stirred by lust at my own funeral. It beat the blandness of the past six months and gave me hope that there was a heaven after all — an absurdity I had discounted during my life.

I considered the possibility that I was experiencing a natural transition during this final, formal exit, and that my family and friends were supposed to look like strangers at this stage of my death. All that talk of reincarnation by my kooky friends may have had more to it than I had believed. Maybe death eradicated the past, wiped the slate clean in preparation for rejoining the herd of living people, with everything and everyone new. Maybe that was the reason why I didn't recognize anyone anymore. Maybe I would go home to a different family after the funeral. Or maybe there was a waiting period for something else to happen, like a Jewish purgatory. More waiting. Always waiting. How was this handled? Was it the same for everyone who died, or were different cases treated differently? Treated? By whom? Perhaps I had been a scientist too long. I decided to cool it and wait for the sermon.

At 11:15 the midget rabbi got up to speak. The top of his head barely cleared the podium, making his voice sound like it was rolling along the ground before working its way up to my ears. He started as for any generic funeral: "We are here today to give our final respects to William Levinson, a dearly beloved husband and father, a professional man of science deeply respected in the community…"

Blah, blah, blah.

This man of God really turned me off. I saw the eyes of the man sitting next to me wander over to the plump woman's daughter. As the minutes went by, I was getting impatient to hear some nice things about myself. After all, I figured it was my last opportunity for that.

The rabbi's talk came to an end, mercifully, and he called Mr. Pinebottom to the podium. Pinebottom walked slowly from his second-row seat and looked quite shaken. I couldn't help wondering if he had a wooden ass, considering his name and the way he walked. He had tears in his eyes and spoke of my love of playing bridge and of his devotion to the temple.

Who's this guy kidding? I don't even know how to play bridge and never played cards. I always thought it a waste of time. And I was not religious. I never stepped foot in the temple except for the high holy days and Allen's Bar-Mitzvah and then Sally's Bat-Mitzvah, and now to attend my funeral.

Pinebottom went on to talk about my contributions as a physicist and…

A physicist? That did it. I looked closely at the congregation and thought how lucky I was that I had never seen these people before. I pinched my hand so hard that I startled myself. I bit my lip until it might bleed. I asked the gentleman on my left what time it was; he checked and said, "11:35." I looked at my own watch, noticed his confusion, and confirmed that I was in the same time zone as he was. Yes, strangers. That's what they were. All of them.

The poor plump widow kept dabbing her drippy puddles with Kleenex. Her pale son sat stiffly, as if he had taken a bath in starch, between his mother and sister, staring without expression at nothing in particular. Who was Dr. Levinson, the physicist, the father of two, the devoted family man and community mensch? May he rest in peace. I had no idea. But I knew who he wasn't. I knew it as well as I knew anything in this world, which I now realized, I was still alive. *He wasn't me.*

I stuck it out for the final statements and a short prayer and then filed in line with the few other miserable people, who were going to the burial. I even went to the widow to pay my respects.

"I'm so sorry," I said, and extended my hand.

Without looking up, she automatically gave me her hand, the one without the wet Kleenex, thank goodness, and I heard a mucus-filled, "Thank you, dear."

Dear? I was doubly glad she was a stranger.

I thought of going to her daughter and giving her a consoling kiss on the cheek, but I have my limits.

I drove home slowly, savoring the moment. I kept seeing Laura's twinkle in my mind, not just her eyes, but her whole being. My heart ached at the thought of her sitting next to me holding my hand all those months I was in a coma. My wife. My best friend.

I loved her.

I wanted to see that purple banner, to touch it, to *feel* it, not again but for the first time. I wanted an M&M. Did "he" call Sally after all? Who is "he"? Why did Allen like black so much? I needed to know. I planned to have dinner with him at his favorite fast-food place on Saturday. I hoped he would be free. Just Allen and me. I couldn't wait.

I cried, without Kleenex. I let the flow fall on my lap. I turned on the radio and bathed in the music. I lowered the window and felt the wind against my face.

"Hello Laura!" I announced as I walked through the front door.

"Why are you here so early?" she called. "It's not even noon. Is anything wrong?"

"Wrong? No. I took the afternoon off. I told Samantha to do the same," I lied.

I told Laura that we only live once, and that it's good to be alive. I asked her to come for a walk with me, just the two of us. The leaves were a tender green. It was the beginning of spring.

She squeezed my hand as we started off towards our favorite path to the canal, just past the cemetery.

Waking Up Dead

When I first overheard two colleagues at work talking about attending my funeral, I thought it was some kind of sick joke. How could I be dead – a corpse, a piece of meat – and at work at the same time?

Well, strange as it may seem, I was dead and at work. Trust me.

Fully engaged in life at 67, I focused on my future, not on dying. How misguided! Expectations don't work out the way they're supposed to. Although it took me time to realize it, I died a week ago. Considering the future now would be as ridiculous as a newborn thinking about the past. My mind is sinking in a quicksand of memories, not plans for next year.

When Rosetta – how lucky I've been to have such a loyal wife – said she couldn't wake me up on Monday morning, March 12, so she called our family physician, who rushed immediately to our home. Dr. Wickett couldn't feel a pulse or breath and pronounced me dead at 8:37. Such precision is typical naïveté of the living. How could anyone know when the exact moment of death occurs when they have never died?

But I can't blame the good doctor. We demarcate our life by sharp boundaries at both ends of the spectrum: "birth" marks the beginning of our colorful life and "death" marks the moment – the instant – life terminates. But when *exactly* are we born? Is it the moment when our head crowns during birth, or do we need to be fully free of our mother? Are we fully alive before we are capable of comprehension and memory? When exactly do we switch from fetus to person?

And when are we completely dead, gone, totally displaced from the world we know? Maybe we can still think or feel or hear for some time after our heart stops and we can no longer breathe. It seems laughable that Dr. Wickett proclaimed me dead exactly at 8:37 a.m. March 12, considering that I was on my way to work. Creating sharp boundaries simplifies our life, I'll give you that – in the same way a caged animal that knows its precise living space has less to worry about than if it was roaming in the precarious jungle.

I learned this past week that death is more porous than I ever imagined. Much more porous. How else could I have felt fine both before and after Dr. Wickett pronounced me dead? Never mind. What anyone believes prematurely about death is irrelevant. I'm grateful I didn't know anything about the death process before I died, not because it would have scared me, but because not knowing made dying an adventure, a learning experience, a denouement for the story of my life.

Why I died remains mysterious. The only known physical anomaly I had was a lesion – a scar that might have impaired transfer of information from one side of my brain to the other – in the corpus callosum, which connects the two hemispheres of my brain. The lesion was discovered many years ago by an MRI investigating possible causes of recurring headaches, but apparently the lesion didn't cause my headaches, which eventually went away as I grew older. The doctors agreed that the lesion was harmless. Why, then, did I die? Well, I can't know everything.

Although unrelated to my death, my daughter Devra thought that my brain lesion explained why I always agreed with both opposing sides of any issue, and she thought that I should have been a diplomat, agreeing with everyone, rather than an objective scientist. "Each of your brain hemispheres has a different viewpoint, Dad," she said. "Your lesion keeps the two hemispheres separate. Of course, you always think both sides are correct." She might say my right hemisphere thinks I'm dead and the left thinks I'm alive at the same time. Nonsense! She's wrong! Having been declared dead, I now know that dead and alive can coexist. So, take that, Devra! What I'm telling you is *not* fiction. I'm not making it up. Every new idea is controversial at first, keeping truth elusive. I'm a scientist, not a diplomat. I'm as honest as they come. Rest assured. You're getting the straight story from a reliable narrator.

When movies show sudden death caused by a bullet or a stroke or a heart attack, it's Hollywood ignorance, or rather good business. True, it appeared to Rosetta and Dr. Wickett that I had crossed the thin life/death boundary at 8:37 on the morning of March 12. However, I didn't know I was dead for another week and I'm still in the "fading from life" stage. I don't know when I'll reach death's finality, but I assume I will eventually.

To help you understand, I am going to document my dying journey here, and correct the misconception that death is incompatible with life.

I woke up on March 12 at 7 a.m., as usual. I stretched, opened my eyes to greet the visual world and started to plan my workday, suffering a low-grade anxiety that always preceded going to the laboratory. Death has not helped me understand my pre-work anxiety, but it no longer matters. It's gone now that I accept that I'm dead.

At approximately 7:20 a.m., I went to the bathroom, turned on the shower and checked if Rosetta was awake yet. She was sitting on my side of the bed looking pale, saying "…are you all right…what's wrong…wake up… you will be late for work."

I replied that I was fine, but she didn't hear me.

Fighting tears, she said, "Oh my god, what's going on? Wake up!"

"I'm fine," I repeated, standing by the door to the bathroom. It was all so strange that I never took the trouble to see if my body was still in bed. Being rushed for an appointment to interview a postdoctoral candidate to join my laboratory, I figured she would realize that I was okay and that would be that. Maybe *she* was not fully awake from a nightmare, or maybe I imagined the scene. I always thought that what I saw and heard and even did was often a blend of reality and interpretation, or imagination.

I grabbed some breakfast, drank an extra cup of coffee and dashed off to the laboratory. Yet, in retrospect, something felt not quite right. I was troubled with Rosetta's strange behavior, and I felt light-headed. I thought I saw Dr. Wickett driving towards my house, but she passed too quickly for me to be sure.

I had no idea that I might be dead. Would you? Would anyone? Of course not. Even the idea sounds ridiculous. Dead and alive at the same time? That's absurd. However, it does fit with the notion that reality and imagination blend.

Let me continue.

"Hello, Dr. Q," said my secretary rather expressionlessly when I arrived at work. Oh, I never mentioned my name. It's Oliver Quantabalinsky. For obvious reasons everyone called me Dr. Q. I was surprised how blandly she greeted me. Usually she sounds more upbeat. In any case, I went into my office as usual for a Monday morning. Everyone seemed friendly and calm – very different from Rosetta that morning.

My emails included four requests from my supervisor that would virtually zap all my time. I needed to provide a detailed account of my discoveries for the last year, list all my postdoctoral fellows for the last five years and state what they were doing now, revise the way we keep our inventory of radioactive chemicals, and finally, state how I was going to adapt my research directions to fit in with the new institute mission. These emails list requests that were typical of the voluminous crap that I had to wade through. I always did my best to comply; however, I wish that I had known then that I was far enough along the pathway to death – that I was at least partially dead – that I didn't need to do any of those things.

I see now, with the distance of death, that these constant bureaucratic demands chipped away layer after layer of my fragile life, exposing the raw core of death.

So, here's another recap. When I awoke on Monday, March 12, my dying had progressed far enough for Rosetta and Dr. Wickett to recognize it for what it was, but the death process had not proceeded far enough yet for my colleagues at work to notice it. The mystery is, how could I have missed recognizing that death was in the process of overtaking my life, despite the signs of that happening?

Why did I dismiss Rosetta's bizarre behavior that morning or the unusual occurrences at work that followed? For example,

I waited in my office until 9:40 for my 9 o'clock appointment to show up, but the person never came. As I try to re-enact that morning, I am uncertain whether my appointment did show up at 9. Maybe she came and neither of us saw each other, or we did and I don't remember. I am so muddled about this, yet I remember clearly other happenings during that fateful morning. I guess that's just an example of how life and death, as remembering and forgetting, blend a lot.

Even though I was dead for Rosetta and Dr. Wickett on Monday morning, the next few days went pretty much the same as in any other week, except for minor irregularities. I worked eight-hour days, went home, had dinner, slept, and carried on as usual. "As usual" is, of course, a lazy phrase in this instance. Nothing is really "as usual." Every day and every action are one of a kind – no two are exactly alike. When we're alive we mistake each "regular" day as no different than a bead in a necklace of similar beads, or a step on a hike along a flat road.

It's too tiring and time-consuming to take note of all the little differences that exist from one day to another – to keep track of all the details – and what a pity that is. It dampens the one thing that truly distinguishes life from death: the uniqueness of each minute, each act, each day.

But back to dying.

There were other signs of my fading life that I failed to recognize that week. Few of my postdoctoral fellows or colleagues made direct eye contact, which was unusual. They smiled at my jokes, but it seemed patronizing, and the postdoctoral fellows often ignored my advice, even in my presence. I sensed my influence receding, but I still wasn't sure. How can I explain it? It was like the difference between being a family member or a guest. The first is permanent; the latter is on borrowed time. The irregularities increased as the week progressed. People stopped showing up for appointments, as had that first 9 o'clock meeting, even if I left a phone message or sent a text reminding them. And sometimes when I was talking, people started a different conversation among themselves.

Rosetta was out when I came home from work that Monday and Tuesday. That too was unusual. I didn't mind preparing my own dinner, but I was scared that Rosetta was leaving me. I asked her on Wednesday if she was angry at me, or what was bothering her. Instead of answering, she gave me the silent treatment.

In retrospect, my passage to death became increasingly evident throughout the week. While on Monday I appeared alive for my peers but not for Rosetta or Dr. Wickett, by Friday it seemed I was pretty much out of the picture at work as well as at home. I wonder if dying occurs at the same rate for everyone or under different circumstances? And here's another puzzling question: if my death was a slow "leakage" of life rather than an abrupt process, when did I start the dying process? Was I equally alive throughout my life as I aged? Probably not. I may have been dying – fading out – slowly for months or years. What I took as growing old, slowing down, losing strength and reflexes and memories, was really the death process. How to distinguish the extent of being alive or being dead? Maybe instead of thinking how old we are, we should think about a changing ratio of alive/dead. Once the ratio passes the tipping point, whatever number that is, we're buried or cremated. I'm beginning to wonder whether the life/death conundrum, as the mind/brain problem, is ever absolute one way or the other.

I'm sorry to ramble this way. I know you're busy living, but I have all the time in the world. Dying is very relaxing.

The turning point for me was on Friday, March 16, when I overheard two colleagues talk about going to my memorial service and funeral on the following Monday morning at 10. Both of these gentlemen work down the hall from my office. Sam said, "I wouldn't miss it for the world." Was he happy to see me dead? Ralph said he would be there too, although he sounded less enthusiastic.

Sam wasn't the only person who wouldn't miss my funeral. Neither would I.

I arrived at 9:50 for my memorial service. I was not religious, yet I was happy that my memorial was in the temple where my kids were a Bar and Bat Mitzvah. The same rabbi presided, even though he was officially retired. I was flattered that he cared enough to come out of retirement to send me on my way.

Many people came to my funeral. Was I more popular than I realized? Since all the seats were already taken by the time I arrived, I stood against the wall on the right side of the chapel along with a few others. Standing room only to see me off! Who wouldn't be happy? There was even a line of people at the door who were instructed to go to the small adjacent chapel where the service would be live-streamed. It would be a lie if I didn't admit pride and pleasure that so many took time out of their busy schedules to come to my funeral.

The seats with green covers in the front of the room were reserved for my family. I think it's likely that Devra, a tree hugger, bless her affected soul, chose green because it reminded her of nature. There was Rosetta of course, my four kids (I have three sons as well as my daughter Devra), their families, my seven grandchildren, even Belinda, my youngest son Ed's daughter who was only 8 months old and nicknamed 'Blunderbuss' because of her extraordinary lung power. I worried a bit that she might let loose during the ceremony. Also present were my brother Brett, his current wife (and surprisingly both of his ex-wives), his three children (one from each wife), my in-laws, and so on. Apparently, I'd gathered family like collecting seashells on the beach.

All my family was dressed in black or dark blue, which depressed me. It was so…dark. Others were dressed more colorfully. One person I swear I'd never seen in my life was even wearing a red jacket with a purple polka-dotted, open-collared shirt. I think that maybe he went to the wrong place by mistake, like Rosetta and I did once when attending her 30th high-school reunion. After eating a good meal and socializing, presumably with former classmates she didn't recognize, we realized that we were at Danny Finkelbaum's Bar Mitzvah, whoever Danny Finkelbaum was. The high school reunion was across the hall. That sort of thing can happen, like beneficial genetic mutations: rare but happy accidents that open new doors.

I could describe the reactions of my family at my funeral in some detail, but it gets morbid and makes me sad. I don't want to dwell on it. I'm not unhappy that I can feel sad even when I'm dead. It means maybe I'm not as dead as I think I am or as I was pronounced.

The sound of gently splashing waves formed a background ambience. I was touched by this gesture since I love the sea – it's so eternal somehow – and I'm passionate about marine biology. Clearly, a lot of thought went into planning my service, and they only had a week, or did something occur even before that? I can assure you that I had nothing to do with the service except be its cause.

The rabbi opened the service with a customary prayer and then began to speak more personally about what a good citizen I had been, a loving husband and parent, a devoted grandparent. The regular spiel. One of the few benefits of a funeral is being beyond reproach. So far, so good. I thought I might even like this funeral, although, of course, being dead was an adjustment. I loved my life, my family and my work, and was determined to enjoy my funeral. I leaned against the wall and decided to believe anything flattering I heard about myself. How many chances does one have for that luxury?

I always felt that my efforts were not sufficiently recognized, which I admit is self-indulgent, and maybe somewhat unfair. I was reasonably successful as a scientist, but I was always plagued with the question, "When is enough?" I used to think "never." How's that for ingratitude? I thought death might break me out of my apparent mediocrity, as it did for Vincent van Gogh, to provide a modest example. So I was excited when I realized that I had been entirely wrong about the abrupt finality of death, and that I still had a chance to hear myself appreciated.

Rosetta did not want to say anything at my funeral (more than understandable), but my kids spoke, and they moved me. They recalled the many wonderful times we had together, collectively and individually. I cried when they talked about our ups and downs, but since I was dead there were no tears. It doesn't do any good to irrigate driftwood. It meant a lot to me that each of my children, even Devra (believe it or not), seemed grateful for all the times that I pestered them about their homework, doing the "right" thing — all that stuff that parents get so much flak for. They didn't seem to remember all the anger, even though I was left feeling like a weed most of the time and was never sure if they forgave me. Devra mentioned how irritated she was when I got unreasonably irritable if she was late, even by a few minutes. She hoped that I would not feel rushed anymore. Everyone in my family, and many in the audience, nodded knowingly when she said this.

Good try, Devra. Your procrastination was always a pain. Never mind. I still love you.

The rabbi got up and said a few words about me, added some mumbo-jumbo, re-anchored his kippah, which kept falling off his head, and turned the service over to the congregation. I assume that he had been asked to be concise. He asked whether anyone wanted to say something about the dearly departed – me. I presumed that the service was about to finish and that my contributions as a scientist would remain as buried as I felt them. What can you do? Let the chips fall as they may…life is short, but death is infinite. Maybe another time.

After 15 to 20 seconds of embarrassing quiet, except for some coughing among the mourners, the man next to me raised his hand and asked to speak. I recognized him as a janitor from my graduate school days at the University of Minnesota.

"Please," acknowledged the rabbi.

"My name is Clarence Silvani and I barely knew the doctor."

I guess my name is irrelevant in the world of the dead.

"He was getting a Ph.D. way back when, and I was the custodian who cleaned the laboratories early in the morning before anyone came to work. I haven't seen the doc since then. He wouldn't have the faintest idea of who I am."

Wrong, Clarence. I recognized you.

"I'll always remember him," said Clarence. "When I read in the newspaper that he passed away, I don't know, I just wanted to come and pay my respects. I don't have any idea what he did, either then or now, before he passed away, that is. It's all above my head. As far as I'm concerned, it don't make much difference. Seems that the important thing is to lead a decent life and have faith – you know what I mean. I've never been too good with words. When I was cleaning up, I saw students, professors, lots of smart guys. I never did get much of a chance to talk to them. Most I ever got out of anyone was a grunt or an empty, "How are you this morning," or "Have a good day." If I tried to tell them how I was when they asked, I'd be speaking to the walls. They never had time to listen to the answer. They didn't care. I can't say that I blamed them much. I didn't care all that much how they were, and that's the truth.

"And then there was the doc. There were many times that he'd be working at that early hour when I came in. He often looked pretty darned tired. He seemed to care a lot about his experiments. As far as I could tell he was busy as all get-out, and he often seemed sort of worried, but when he asked me, 'How're you doing this morning,' he waited for the answer. At first, I didn't say much, but I remember once he said, 'Tell me, Clarence – is everything okay with you? You look like something is bothering you.'

"The doc remembered my name. Can you imagine? The first time it nearly brought tears to my eyes. I didn't let him know that, of course. It was like I suddenly became more important.

"I told him that I was okay, but my wife had this terrible pain in her joints and couldn't sleep, and that I had a hard time making the mortgage payments. Sometimes we talked about the Vikings, you know – the football team. I loved the Vikings; they made a winner out of me. The doc knew as much about the players as I did – actually more. That's about it. I never even asked about him. I don't know, I was just the custodian and all. I never forgot the doc. He gave me self-respect. I just wanted to come here today and give him my respects."

Clarence stopped speaking and stared straight ahead. I wanted to scream, "Here I am, Clarence, and thanks." I was standing right next to him and he didn't know it. Maybe he did – at least I'd like to think he felt some sort of my presence, since he looked directly at me for a moment.

Next, a woman at the other end of the room stood and began to speak.

"I was Dr. Reiter's secretary for ten years. Dr. Reiter worked on the third floor while Dr. Q was on the second floor, so we didn't have much to do with each other. I saw Dr. Q from time to time when I went down to see his secretary Patsy. Patsy liked working for him, although she did tell me that he didn't pay much attention to bureaucratic details, which made her job more difficult. One day I was walking down the hall and Dr. Q stopped me and said, 'Helen, everything all right?' That's all. It was like he sensed something, like he did for Clarence. I did have a problem. Since my defenses were down, I started telling him about my difficulties, and he listened. He asked if I wanted to go to his office where it would be more private. I was embarrassed, but agreed, and we talked for about ten minutes. I told him that my 6-year-old son was not getting along at school and was depressed and anxious. My friends always gave me a pep talk and said that he would outgrow it, told me about their kids, said I was a great mom, that kind of thing. But Dr. Q understood how difficult this was for me and gave me the name of a psychologist, a friend of his. I know that doesn't sound so fantastic, but believe me, if it wasn't for him and that psychologist, my son may not have become the successful banker and family man he is today. Thank you, Dr Q. I hope that you can hear me."

And she sat down.

Yes, you're right, it's not so fantastic, but you're welcome. I remember the episode. I hardly gave it a second thought. It wasn't such a big deal to recommend a friend to someone in need. It's all in a day's work, as I see it.

Another person rose.

"I…I…I just wanted to say something, but actually it's kind of silly, but anyway, I want to say it. My name is Dr. Robert Hall and I'm the pharmacist where Dr. Q got his prescriptions filled. He was always in a rush, always said that I had to fill it quickly because he had a lot to do. Seems he even rushed to die. But there's one thing about him that was special. Lots of doctors snub us pharmacists like we're just some kind of commercial tool or something. But after I talked for a few minutes to him, when he had time that is, I always felt good about myself. It didn't really matter what we talked about – sports, cars, work, the weather, just about anything. I don't have any idea why it was, but afterwards, I felt a little more significant. That's it. He made me feel significant. I tried to get his prescriptions as quickly as I could, so he didn't have to wait too long."

Bob Hall is right about that, I was always in a hurry, and that's because the guy was slow as molasses. I'm happy that he felt significant after talking to me, but don't ask me why.

When Professor Martin Hildebrand, my long-term colleague from Yale, stood up I thought I would finally hear something substantive about myself. He's one of the most respected scientists in the country with all sorts of honors – a superstar. I remember leaning forward to make sure I heard every word that Martin said.

"I've known Oliver for over thirty years," he said.

We were on first name basis, unlike the others who spoke.

"We met first at a scientific meeting in Italy and then our wives became friends. We saw each other socially as well as professionally. He had an easy-going personality, rather laid back, but I do think he cared a lot about his work. Oliver always made things easy for me. When I called, he called back immediately if I left a message. If I needed a letter for something, he would write it without delay. He was a steady guy. I never mistook his willingness to help for subservience. He'll be missed."

Professor Hildebrand sat down looking like he'd fulfilled his obligation.

Subservience! Who does Martin think he is? Laid back? A steady guy? Does he think that makes me a good scientist? What about the time he didn't know how to interpret his data until I figured it out, and then he published it without even acknowledging me? I've had it! Martin seems to have cared for me to some extent, when he wasn't caring for himself that is, and he did come to my funeral. But…what he didn't say screamed in my ears, loud and clear and frankly, I'm pissed! Suddenly I feel alive again, and it's exhausting. Maybe it's better to be dead.

A tentative voice then came from along the wall. I didn't recognize the voice. Who was this guy?

"I never met Dr. Q…" started the stranger.

What the heck does he want to say?

"But I am here today because of him."

Of course. Everyone goes to a funeral because of the dead guy.

"I came from Russia and the immigration department was about to deport me due to an expired visa. I needed a green card to stay in this country. I came with my family and it was very scary, very difficult for us. Since I study eyes, like Dr. Q, and he was well known, I sent him an email and asked him if he would write a letter of recommendation and help me stay in this country. I couldn't believe it when he responded within a day, a busy man like that. He asked me to send him any information that would help him know who I was and what he could say about me. A few days later he emailed me and said he had written a strong letter on my behalf and wished me luck. Soon after I was accepted for a green card. I'm sure that was because of him.

"Today I am an associate professor at Boston University and a U.S. citizen with an American family. I wrote to Dr. Q to thank him, but I still never met him."

For whatever reason, this particular eulogy got to me. My sarcastic streak was left floating in the breeze. I was filled with genuine pride that I had helped this man. I wanted to hug my Russian – now American – "friend."

Without warning, Martin Hildebrand, and science, and ambition all flashed through my mind, all mixed together in no specific order, and left me disoriented for a moment. How surprising to discover by the offhand comments of a stranger I never met, who I really was. Martin's image faded and was replaced by that of Clarence, and Dr. Reiter's secretary, and the Russian immigrant, and even the pharmacist Robert Hall. I felt at peace for the first time in my life, not because I was dead, but because I had lived.

The rabbi returned to the bimah and gave a short prayer. He invited everyone to the burial in the cemetery outside of the temple. A small group came, as I did, of course.

I knew most of the people at the cemetery but there were also some that I swear I had never ever laid eyes on. I didn't know whether dying erased my memories of some people, or whether there was another explanation. I always had trouble recognizing faces, so maybe I did know everyone. Or perhaps they were strangers I had helped as I did the grateful Russian. There were pitifully few scientists who took the trouble to go outside in the cold for the actual burial, except for my students, who looked genuinely sad. Martin was not there.

I watched myself slip into the casket involuntarily – it just happened – and then I was lowered into the ground by a small crane. My world was black now, and very quiet. I worried that such cramped conditions would be claustrophobic, but at the moment that didn't bother me. Dying was indeed an adventure. Each happening was a new experience.

I wondered how I would know when my death is finished. Maybe it already is. Will I come back to life, or remain partially alive forever, whatever forever is? I never believed in reincarnation, but who knows? I'm no longer sure about anything.

I still don't believe in heaven or hell, but if I'm wrong, I hope it's heaven.

It's all impressive and ordinary at the same time. Life and death. Maybe they're both the same thing and special in the same way that everyone is special: elite by commonality. Ironic.

Let the chips fall where they may. One never knows, does one?

Goodbye. Unfortunately, I won't see you later, or will I?

Death by Drowning

I first met my father when he was in prison and I was a 30-year-old mother. I wished I could tell Mom, a nurse, how sorry I am that I ever doubted her, but that was impossible, since a hit-and-run driver killed her five years ago when she was on vacation crossing a street in Paris during a hard-earned and rare vacation. I am a single mother as well, with an adorable two-year-old daughter, Rachel. But that's where my similarity with Mom ends. She was abandoned after a one-night stand with a man she had just met, although she said she abandoned him. In any case, she was more forgiving than I am. I'm divorced from a stockbroker with a roving eye for sexy women. At least he was good at making money, so I am getting regular child support. That's more than Mom ever got.

Although I blamed my father for his neglect, I felt more secure and grounded after meeting him. Suddenly I had a real live father – a Dad – and hopefully a supporter, despite his earlier absence. I loved Mom, of course, but she couldn't replace an absent father. I never knew what to tell my peers when they asked, "Are your parents divorced? Where's your dad? How often do you visit him?" I was ashamed to say I was an accident – the progeny of a single night with a stranger: that I had never met my father and probably never would. Of course I resented him, but I also missed the father I never knew, the man who never hugged me, the dad I never cuddled with or twisted around my little finger and said in a sweet flirtatious way, "Please, pretty please," to get my way, as my girlfriends did with their dads. He even made me resent Mom when she had to walk me down the aisle instead of him.

How could Mom forgive him? It wasn't right.

Mom told me more when I was a teenager than I'm letting on, though I was never sure what to believe. Because the story didn't sound like her at all.

She told me she met my father, Ricardo Sztein – a scientist considerably older than her – in a discothèque in the romantic Riviera on the Côte d'Azur. He was attending a conference and must have been sort of a big deal, since he gave the keynote lecture at the meeting. When I pressed Mom for more details about him, she said, "I only knew him that one night," and then blushed self-consciously, swearing that she'd never slept with anyone else even close to the nine months before I was born.

"Did you ever tell him you were pregnant?" I asked.

"No. He was married and said that he had never cheated on his wife before. And I was not the type of person to sleep with someone I had just met – only that once. When I woke up in the morning he was gone. I had no idea that our folly would lead to my pregnancy. He doesn't know you exist."

"And…?" I wanted more facts. "Did he have kids?"

"No, although he told me his wife, I think her name was Lillian, wanted to have children, but they never came," she said. "There's nothing else, Juliette. I never contacted him. It was my fault too, as much as his. But having you wasn't a fault. It was the best thing I ever did!"

I still couldn't forgive her for not trying to let him know he had a daughter – me! Sweet Juliette. Not letting him know wasn't even fair to him.

Mom had saved a poster from the conference with his picture, so I knew what he looked like at the time they met. An Argentinean who lived in America, he was darker, more like me, than my light-skinned mother, and had high cheekbones. Mom said he was very talkative that night and said how much he loved doing basic research in biology, but the pressure to do medical research frustrated him. He kept saying, "I'm a basic scientist, not a physician. I love health, not disease; life, not death."

"He was special, Juliette, one of a kind."

I think that Mom fell in love with him that night and never got over it, although she denied that. When I asked her more specifically what was so special about him, she didn't dwell on his looks or charm or any of the usual things that win people over. "It was jellyfish, Juliette, believe it or not. Jellyfish!"

"Jellyfish? What do you mean?"

"He wasn't just a scientist," she said. "He was a story-teller and an artist at heart. When he talked about his work with jellyfish, which he had been studying, he drifted to a private universe, a hidden kingdom," my mother recalled. "Even his movements became a combination of flowing and jerky. Jellyfish had eyes, he said, and he wanted to know what they saw and how that affected their behavior. He appeared to be floating in another world with different rules and meaning, or more accurately an underwater paradise, quiet and free. He dreamed that he was among jellyfish, as if he had joined their society. Oh Juliette. I wish you had heard him. Then you would understand. It didn't matter to me what was true scientifically. How would I know anyway? He literally swept me off my feet. I had never met anyone like him."

"Mom," I said, "all that's fine, though a bit melodramatic. How much did you drink that night? Never mind. No matter what you say, he *abandoned* you! Doesn't that make you mad?"

"Sometimes. Sure. I don't know. He mentioned his wife several times and felt guilty to be with me. It wasn't as if he abandoned me, as you keep saying, or you, since he didn't know about you. I consented to our encounter, knowing he was going back to his home. He didn't know that I became pregnant. How many times do I have to say that?"

"Maybe," I said, "but still…He wasn't the first married man to have an illegitimate kid. He could have checked with you at some point. It seems he *was* rather a spineless jellyfish."

When I was 23, I read the following headline in the New York Times: *Ricardo Sztein to Serve Ten Years for Misuse of Government Funds*. The accompanying story suggested that he was the same man.

"I'm sad, but not surprised," Mom said when I told her about the story. "He had said that no one would believe him. I guess he was right."

I was dumbfounded. It was bad enough to be the daughter of a father who didn't know I existed, but now I was also the child of a convict! What in the world could he have done that was so bad studying jellyfish? He didn't sound like a criminal. I was curious, but I didn't pursue the matter further. Neither did Mom. I blame both of us for that. He went to jail, and I became a nurse, married, had Rachel and divorced. Then Mom was killed in that tragic hit-and-run accident. The French police never found the driver who killed her.

Eventually I decided to visit my father in jail. I blamed Mom all those years for never looking him up, and I didn't want to do the same thing. Also, his ten-year sentence wouldn't last forever – then it might have been very difficult if not imposible to find him. Would he confirm Mom's story? I had to meet him, to see him in the flesh, to ask him questions. Later, if I still doubted that he was my father, I could get a genetic test, if he agreed.

I called the prison and they told me visiting hours were Saturdays from 2 to 4 p.m.

When I arrived at the correctional center my hand was shaking so much I could hardly push the button to announce my presence. I was buzzed in and the heavy steel door opened slowly, mechanically, gears grinding, with no one to greet me. I found my way to the office at the end of the dingy hall. It was an experience in ghastly gray: there were no windows, bare cinderblock walls, two naked incandescent light bulbs on the relatively low ceiling, nothing to absorb the sound of my echoing footsteps, no color, no human touch, no hope. Even the smell seemed a dull-musty gray.

I'd never been so nervous in my life as when I stepped into that sequestered, depressing world.

"Here to see inmate 2231?" asked the guard when I gave his name. "Who's asking for him?" Then he noted curtly, "That guy never had a visitor before."

I was stumped. He didn't know me or that he had a daughter. What should I say?

"Tell him a very special visitor is here to see him," I said.

"That's it? No name"

"Right. No name."

The guard eyed me suspiciously, asked again for my name and ID, checked my purse, and escorted me to the visitors' room. Several inmates were speaking with visitors at small tables. At least this wasn't a high security prison with murderers and the like, so the prisoners could meet directly with their visitors, who were mostly family, I presumed.

I inhaled the stale air and waited. A few minutes later, Ricardo came in with the guard, looked at me quizzically and walked cautiously to the table where I sat.

"Who are you?" he asked politely.

"I'm Juliette," I said, my voice cracking a bit. He stared at me and I looked down at my feet self-consciously.

"Are you a scientist? Do you study jellyfish maybe?"

With this question, he suddenly looked more alert, so I asked, "Is that who you would like to meet, a scientist who does research on jellyfish?'

He looked at me curiously.

"I'm not a scientist," I said, not waiting for him to answer and sorry to disappoint him. I didn't resent him any more at that moment. "I'm…I'm…that is, I'm someone special in your life, but not a scientist. I don't know anything about jellyfish."

"Special?"

I couldn't come outright and say that I was his daughter.

"Remember Monique?" I thought he might remember my mother's name.

He blanched, turned as white as I've ever seen anyone lose color. I was scared he would faint. He just stared at me with big brown eyes, his mouth slightly open. We looked at each other for a few seconds, which felt like half an hour. His surprise confirmed it for me. No one would react like that after just hearing Mom's name. Suddenly I felt we were on the same playing field, father and daughter, genetically similar, complements of each other. In a strange way, I was at home in that prison with my convict dad I'd never met before.

"Monique was my mother." There, that said it all. Now he must have known that I was his daughter, or at least that I might be. But he didn't say a word. His left hand trembled, droplets of sweat appeared on his forehead.

Finally, "Monique, you say? Your *mother*? Really?"

"Yes. Remember her?"

"You said she 'was' your mother. What do you mean 'was'?"

"A hit-and-run driver killed her in Paris five years ago."

"Oh my god!" he said, with such surprise that I felt I was learning it for the first time myself.

"I think what Mom told me is true. I'm your daughter."

I didn't know what he was thinking. Did he believe me? I went on and repeated what Mom had told me: that she had worn her pink skirt the night they met, that he had remarked on the curl in the corner of her upper lip, that he worked on jellyfish, that they had gone back to his hotel after a few too many drinks, that he was gone when she awoke in the morning, that she never saw him again.

"Yes," he muttered. "That curl on her lip, and all that pink."

Mom had told the truth. The puzzle was complete. I had Mom's golden, curly hair, but his earthy hue, not Mom's milk-white complexion. I had his high cheekbones and small feet and coffee-colored eyes, nothing like Mom's blue-gray eyes, and I squinted when self-conscious, just like I saw him squint.

I don't know what possessed me to say next what I did, but I blurted out, "She loved you." Then I blushed.

He understood, and then he cried, and so did I, and in my mind, so did the rest of humanity.

"I'm your daughter. You're my father."

"It seems so. She never told me."

"You never contacted her. Why not?"

He looked crushed for a moment, then said, "I'm sorry."

"So am I."

"She never married, your mother?"

"No."

"My wife Lillian always wanted kids. As much as I loved her, I'm glad she's dead. Oh god, forgive me, but at least she'll never know this. A kid with another woman."

"You know the slight curl on the left side of her upper lip?"

"Yes, I loved it," he said.

"You'll love it again on Rachel, your granddaughter."

This was almost too much. His eyes darted around the room, he breathed faster, he tensed his thigh muscles and rubbed the back of his neck. "I have a whole family!"

"Yes," I said, proud to make him so happy.

We talked awhile and I gave him a photo of Rachel. He held it in both hands as he would precious art. I'll never be able to relive that moment when three generations blended for the first time.

Suddenly he started talking rapidly, like Mom said he had with her that night.

"It was a solitary, impulsive act many years ago," he said, and then confessed to having kept it secret from his wife. "I loved Lillian too much to hurt her." He told me again how much she had wanted children and grandchildren, but she was plagued with miscarriages. "That I have a daughter with another woman is cruelly unfair," he said, but relented when he saw me wince.

"But you're a gift," he added quickly. "An accidental family," he said

He looked tenderly at Rachel's photograph and smiled softly, lovingly.

I asked him why he was in jail.

"It doesn't make sense," he said. "It was my jellyfish research, which was considered misuse of government funds and not serious research for medical advances. The country was going through an economic crisis. They said I was indulging my curiosity at the expense of taxpayers. Ridiculous. It takes time before many little discoveries add up to something important and sometimes lead to a whole new way to think of nature. The path from discovery to application is never straight and generally surprising. Before my studies, everyone thought of jellyfish as a mass of slimy stuff. No! That's wrong! I showed they are more. They communicate, they probably have emotions, they may even think, in a jellyfish kind of way, of course. There's so much more to do. But maybe someone else…"

Poor, disheartened man. I wondered if I felt then what Mom did that night in the discothèque. I felt disoriented, as if switching roles wth her, reliving a scene I had never witnessed, a false sense of *déjà vu*. Maybe the only way to understand another person is to become that person, as impossible as that may seem – to leap across one's boundaries, to invade someone else's space.

I pushed him further. "What did you discover about those jellyfish that you thought was so important?"

His demeanor brightened as suddenly as a rainbow paints the sky when a dark rain cloud moves aside in deference to the summer sun.

"Oh, what a wonderful time it was in La Parguera in Puerto Rico, where I lived my dream to immerse myself in nature and peek into the world of jellyfish." His voice quivered with distant excitement. "Where to begin. The sweet, humid smell of the salty air, how I loved it, free of silly obligations, the mangrove swamp, all those mysterious animals, universes within universes under our very noses, and we don't see a thing."

"What animals? What mysterious universes? What don't we see?" I was lost.

"Crabs and worms and starfish – all the invertebrates – jellyfish especially – all the obscure animals that hardly anyone cares about, as if they were not alive or had no souls. But they are living, like we are living, and they know as little of us as we do of them, and, like us, don't care. We're so ignorant, just like they are."

Was he mad? And then I remembered how Mom had said he seemed to escape to another world when he had talked about jellyfish.

Seconds later he continued, more slowly, and with a certain sadness.

"When I felt lonely in the laboratory, especially at night, the jellyfish in the bowls kept me company. I seemed to enter their world, to become a jellyfish myself! In those moments of deepened consciousness, I saw, felt, sensed what's it's like to be a jellyfish. It wasn't a dream or some kind of spaced-out state. It was real. How extraordinary, how peaceful, how different, how comforting…it's beyond description. I'm sure the jellyfish saw me too. Because jellyfish have eyes and can see."

"Mom said you told her that jellyfish have eyes, and it also was in the newspaper article about your trial."

He nodded.

"Jellyfish have wonderful eyes, complex ones like ours," he continued, "with a lens and cornea and retina. I'm sure they have a brain of sorts as well. Jellyfish recognize each other and have distinct personalities, I'm convinced. My experiments showed that. How could jellyfish do all that without a brain?"

I listened without interrupting him.

"It's Galileo all over again, as my lawyer Sophia told the jury. It was the Middle Ages again, but this time it was about elevating the lowly jellyfish rather than demoting the heavenly bodies. Why does Man always resist reconfiguring his place in the universe?"

"I don't know," I said, not sure what he meant.

"Never mind. No one knows. I couldn't really inhabit the jellyfish universe," he concluded. "It's the *No Trespassing* law of nature, which makes other species so mysterious to us. We are locked into our own boundaries. The jellyfish eyes are strategically placed so they see all around themselves at the same time. We wouldn't know how to handle that much information. I even had strong data that jellyfish could see evolution – the past. Isn't that amazing? But I don't think anyone believed it. Jellyfish seem more advanced than us in some ways. Who knows? Sorry. Lillian would tell me to stop rambling."

The guard entered the visitor's room. "Time's up," he said.

Leaving him was awkward, but I was ready. Bombarded with information myself, I needed my own space.

"Well, goodbye for now," I said, leaning in in his direction self-consciously. We didn't hug, but our hands touched. Although he was my father, he was still a stranger.

"Yeah, goodbye," and then he said my name for the first time. "Juliette."

"When can I come back?" I asked.

"Whenever you want. I have no plans to leave."

I smiled. "Next Saturday then," and I left.

I was happy and relieved. I wanted to tell Rachel she had a grandfather, but she was too young now to understand. The telling could wait.

When I returned the following Saturday, the office guard told me inmate 2231 wasn't doing well. He had missed a few meals during the week. One of the guards who had taken a liking to him brought him a sandwich, since he hadn't eaten all day. This morning the sandwich was still there, with just one bite gone.

"I'll go tell him you're here," the guard said. "Wait for me."

Five minutes later he returned looking confused and said that Ricardo was walking in slow circles. He asked if I could come to his cell. It was against regulations, but the guard said he would make an exception if I kept it quiet.

The first thing I noticed when I entered the cell was Rachel's picture taped to the wall, but it felt strange to see my sweet daughter next to the photograph of a woman I presumed was his deceased wife, Lillian. Rachel was my Mom's granddaughter, not Lillian's. I needed to give him a picture of my Mom, which I would bring next time.

I sat on the cot. I thought he would be happy to see me, but he just kept circling.

"Hi," I said, trying to be cheerful.

He kept pacing, swaying his arms effortlessly.

"What's bothering you," I asked. "Are you all right?"

He gazed at me as if I were a creature he had never seen before. It was scary and I felt like an intruder. His shoulders moved up and down in rhythm with his legs, and his head bobbed like a buoy on a gentle sea. He peered here and there, touched this and that, and stopped to stare at the pictures of Lillian and Rachel. I felt increasingly uncomfortable and out of place.

"Do you want me to leave?"

He stopped walking and shook his head indicating I shouldn't leave, but I wasn't sure. I stayed.

He started walking again, this time in short mechanical pulses, advancing two steps with each pulse, very regularly. He stopped in the middle of the room and stood motionless. "I'm coming, Lillian," he said. "I miss you so."

"Do you see Lillian?" I asked, with a voice so faint that I was uncertain whether I had actually spoken or just imagined the words.

"See how her tentacles move in synchrony, how she drifts effortlessly through the water, how she beckons me to join her?" He then swayed his hips slowly side to side.

"Are you swimming with the...jellyfish...*Dad?*" There, I'd said it. Dad. I would not die without having called him that at least once. I felt complete.

"The water is cool," he said. "I'm buoyant, free."

Watching him made me feel weightless, as if I too was suspended in water. I retrieved a faded picture of Mom from my purse. She was in her favorite pink skirt and smiling, with the slight curl of her upper lip evident.

I showed him the picture.

"Monique," he whispered. I understood that he had to whisper. Mom was his secret. Lillian mustn't hear.

"Here, take it," I said, offering him the picture - my only copy. "Please. You can have it."

"Poor Monique," he said, looking at Mom's picture. But he didn't take it out of my hand.

"Are the jellyfish still around you?" I asked.

"Oh, yes," he said returning to his imaginary world. "There are even more now." His voice was so soft that I had to strain to hear him. "There are many little ones – babies – that just arrived." He looked at Mom's picture again, still in my hand.

"I love you all," he said.

I didn't know if he meant the jellyfish, or Lillian, my Mom and Rachel – and maybe even me. Then his eyes locked into mine, forming a tunnel for his soul to transfer into me, or perhaps mine into his. His knees buckled as if his bones were dissolving, and he folded slowly, ever so slowly, to the floor, more a blanket than a body. He wrapped his arms around an imaginary something, and I heard him say, so quietly I couldn't be sure, "Rachel."

I knelt beside him on the floor. He looked peaceful, and I imagined a smile carved deeply in his face. He was stone still. I called out to the guard.

"He's gone," said the guard when he failed to feel a pulse in his wrist or a breath when he placed his face next to my father's mouth. "I'm sorry, Miss."

I closed his eyes gently with my hand and brushed my fingers along his cheek – and recoiled abruptly. What unexpected slime! I wiped my hand on my blouse and sat back down on the cot, riveted on his corpse. Was this really happening? I closed my eyes for a few seconds looking for the jellyfish he had seen and spoken to, but I saw nothing unusual. Of course, there were no jellyfish.

"Has he changed in any way the last few days?" I asked the guard. The other guard had told me he had, but I wanted confirmation.

"Well, he was a loner," said the guard. "But, yes, he did seem different this week. He barely ate, and this morning he kind of floated around the room and – how to say it? – appeared disconnected – you know what I mean? – like he was from a different planet."

"A different planet?" I muttered to myself. I was trying to put it all together.

"That's right."

"He was doing the same with me now. Was his so-called 'floating' smooth or jerky?"

The guard looked perplexed.

"Did he glide or did he kind of pulsate? Did he move by jerks, like a jellyfish might swim? I'm just checking what you saw. I know it's a strange question."

"A jellyfish?" asked the guard, as if he'd misunderstood. He looked at me strangely.

"Yes," I insisted, "a *jellyfish*!" I was impatient and growing flustered. "Did he *pulsate* around the room, as if he was acting like a jellyfish?"

"I wouldn't know about that."

"Can we do an autopsy? I need to know why he died."

"It could be anything," said the guard. "He might have had a stroke or heart attack. He was pretty old, in his mid-eighties, I guess. Things happen."

I didn't buy it. "Did he take drugs?"

"Impossible! We check for narcotics constantly here, and you have been his only visitor. I'm sorry, but we aren't required to do autopsies on prisoners when they die unless the circumstances warrant it or their families insist."

"But I'm his daughter!" I said. "His *daughter*, do you understand? I share his genes, I'm partly him, and he's partly me. I'm his daughter and I want an autopsy."

The guard stepped back a pace, surprised by my sudden outburst.

"Yes, yes, of course, ma'am. If you're his daughter, I'll speak to the warden."

Two days later the autopsy report eliminated heart attack and stroke. There was no evidence of drugs or poison, consistent with what the guard had said. But there were two unexplained findings. The first was a thin, mucous-like slime covering his skin, consistent with what I had felt. And the second was even more peculiar: his lungs were filled with water.

"Water-filled lungs? Mucous-like slime? What does that mean?"

The doctor who performed the autopsy shrugged. "I've never seen this before. I have no idea about the slime. As for the water in his lungs, well, that's consistent with someone who drowned. But that can't be possible."

"Impossible?" I asked.

For a moment, I imagined I saw jellyfish drifting in water. Though they quickly disappeared. I had the fleeting understanding, just for a second, that it might have been possible – that it might *be* possible – to drift past the *No Trespassing* sign my father had described, and to enter a different universe.

My father had tried to enter the jellyfish universe and failed. I saw that clearly, in a sudden epiphany that I couldn't prove, but believed was right. Not everything can be proved; some things just are. My father couldn't poke through his boundary and escape his loneliness by becoming a jellyfish any more than he could bring Lillian or my Mom back to life. Yes, he drowned, but in air, with no sea in sight. Because he couldn't become a jellyfish any more than a jellyfish could become a human.

Then I thought of Mom and the *No Trespassing* confinement. I could never escape my mind to inhabit hers as my own, or to enter Dad's conflicts as he suffered through them, just as he couldn't understand or transform into a jellyfish.

"Poor Dad," I said half-aloud.

"Excuse me?" asked the doctor.

"Never mind."

Sometimes there's no simple way to explain the truth.

Tip-Top LUNCHEO
SODAS · TOASTED SANDWICH
FOUNTAIN S
JUMBO
MALTED
MILK
5¢
BREAKFAST SPECIAL
COFFEE 10¢
5¢

Mr. Blok

Approximately 70 years ago, my father wrote a novel, titled *Mr. Blok*, which has never yet been published. Finally, after languishing all these years in manuscript form, it will soon be published by Adelaide Books. I had never read it myself until this year, 2019, when I retrieved it from its state of suspended animation. I was taken aback, but not all that surprised, to discover that it contained themes that echo those I have explored in the preceding stories, in which I imagine a type of transition between life and death – a dream-like state of partially alive and partially dead simultaneously. Papa's novel and my fantasy short stories shared a similar surrealistic ambiguity of being alive and dead.

The novel opens with Mr. Blok in a ditch and immediately raises the questions of whether the story is a dream or a factual account.

"Mr. Blok thought it was a dream; but he must have been wrong. He walked through the Square one night and arriving at 20th Street, fell into a ditch they were digging for sewer pipes or something."

As my father's story progresses, the adventures of Mr. Blok unfold, and at the end he falls once again into a ditch. Now the confusion of being between dream and reality evolves into an ambiguous state of being alive or dead, and considers a certain similarity between the two states, implying a blurry transition between them. While it is impossible to provide a precise scientific rationale for being both alive and dead in these tales of fantasy, I was struck by how my father had played with surrealistic ideas about life and death, as have I so many decades later. Could this be viewed as a generational continuity between a dead father and a living son – a different sort of mystery that sees how fantastic thoughts die with the parent and yet live on with the son?

I ask you to consider this yourself.

Excerpt from the last chapter of Mr. Blok

"Oh, oh, …isn't it hard to make a stop when on the move?" he asked himself, panting and turning to the right… "Oh God! Stop me," he prayed. "Have mercy." He saw a tricycle coming towards him. Was it a colored boy speeding so madly? He felt a hard blow from the front wheel and hit the ground and rolled into a ditch. A sharp pain passed almost instantly.

"Father, father," he heard the boy cry. "He is not hurt, father. He's just very old."

Blok opened his eyes.

"Mr. Blok," he heard the man say. Blok recognized him. "Mitchell Wrinkly?"

There was a long silence.

Mr. Wrinkly said, "No, son, Mr. Blok is not old – he is dead! He's surely dead. Let's get out of here before someone comes."

Blok heard them hustle away. "It's a pity. I would have liked to see him," he thought, with great sadness.

Lying on his back in the mud, soft and warm, with his eyes closed, in the marvelous quietness made him feel almost grateful and glad. How amazingly simple it is to be dead. The transition is so painless, it is hardly perceptible. "Oh, nature is kind," he admired quietly. "Such a short distance from life and such quietness. If people knew, they would never be frightened of death, never – never. Perhaps later I will find a greater difference on this side – the side of death – if there is any. No wonder so many people don't know they are dead.

"It is good to get rid of one's body when the best in one remains. I can still think...muse...oh, if only there is such a thing here. When was I killed? Since when am I dead? Hmmm, utterly unimportant. It's like fainting. A drunkard who passes out must feel the same. Hm...no...no...he can't. A real true death is a sober death which can reason and remember. I can. With many beautiful recollections, the life of a corpse can be fine."

He heard steps overhead. "Someone is coming to welcome me here."

"Hello...blo...blo...greetings."

Mr. Blok did not answer. He listened.

"If there is such a thing as hell you will not know it. Congratulations!" the voice continued. "I can always tell one new boarder from the other."

Mr. Blok could neither see nor speak.

"The ditch – grave – even the urn after cremation are recognized channels to enter this place, but I was not so lucky." The voice began to speak in fast tempo. "I came straight from the electric chair and before I could say blo...blo...I became Short Wave. Blasted Cabbage! What a life! Jerking convulsively in fabulous

speed without a second of rest, intercepting messages, codes, mostly broken parts of them, sent in queer languages, delivering them God knows where. Finally, I am going to be promoted to Long Wave – it's a cinch."

Blok heard steps vanishing into ethereal distance. He turned on his side. "What was that? Queer!" He felt pain in his legs. He moved his arm. "Am I alive after all? Strange." He took a deep breath. "Oh, my chest, my neck!" He opened his eyes wide on the dribbling wall. "Am I again in the ditch? Where is Wrinkly?" He remembered. He tried to get up, but his feet seemed soft and joint-less, stuck in the mud. He burrowed his hands in the ground and forced his elbows and arms to lift his heavy back until he could sit leaning against the wall. While resting and composing himself, he listened to the steps of people passing on the sidewalk overhead. "They trample on me. Not these. These steps are light. Must be a nice person – a woman. Why doesn't she stop and look into the ditch? Every step has a different character – a different meaning. They are more telling than faces. They did not learn to lie."

He tried to visualize each person. All of a sudden, he wanted to listen to his own steps. "I must get out of here. Didn't Wrinkly say exactly the same words. Hmmm, he ran away from murder." He looked at his soiled suit. "I must be quite a sight," he mur-mured half-jokingly. "Brainy and interesting men are seldom good looking." With this thought, he stood up and brushing dirt from his jacket tried to climb out of the ditch. After many attempts he finally emerged and supporting himself against the wall of a building, was glad to rest for a while.

The passerby hardly paid any attention to him. Mr. Blok took indifference for kindness. "There are multitudes of truly fine people in this world," he said to himself, slowly advancing toward the Square. It was a beautiful starless evening.

He must have had a smile on his face, for a lady, as if in answer, smiled also. When she passed, Mr. Blok turned and watched her fragile and anxious figure, as though in search of friendliness, disappear into the dark. Strolling along the Square, Blok's thoughts touched only vaguely on the recent occurrences, and his mind was not preoccupied with the immediate needs of the day. "I feel like a newborn, and maybe I am. Don't those who really live, live anew? Feeling and seeing the new in the old? They never know boredom."

What's Alive?

At first glance, alive is clearly distinguished from dead; alive and dead are mutually exclusive states. Yet, defining the specific traits required for life, becomes less clear. There is no known magic, vital substance that gives life to an inanimate object. No touch from God is necessary to explain life. Almost a hundred years ago, Erwin Schrodinger argued in his classic book – *What is Life?* – that life can be understood in physical/chemical terms. This has turned out to be consistent with the modern, reductionist view of biology, where DNA is king – the mastermind template – and its RNA and protein products the vassals – the workhorses – of life. Life can be viewed as a manifestation of chemistry and physics.

Is what appears dead always dead? Microbial spores can remain dormant – appear lifeless – for many, many years until germination ensues with changing conditions. Does that mean there can be transformation from death to life by a change in external conditions? What's the difference between dead and dormant, except that the latter is reversible? Why is a "lifeless" spore not dead? How many other life forms appear dead, or exist at questionable in-between states? What about viruses, small packets of genetic material tightly wrapped in a proteinaceous sheath? Viruses can't do a thing on their own; the tiny inert particles – too small for the naked eye to see – wait inertly, that's all they do. When the opportunity arises, they slip into a bacterium or a cell, depending on the nature of the virus, and exploit the host to their own advantage to replicate and replicate and replicate, over and over, many thousands of times. The massive reproduction of virus far outdoes the solitary nature of reproduction of mammals. The virus, now suddenly alive, violates its host and gains control by placing one or more of its genes into the host's gene pool, or steals a gene or two from its hapless victim to pass on to other victims. Is a virus alive or dead? Or both, depending on circumstances?

Okay, I admit, I'm letting my scientific background interfere with essential general questions. In contrast to microbial spores or viruses, we worry about ourselves, egocentrics that we are.

As I age with slowing reflexes and diminishing physical strength, and as I watch, sadly, family members, friends and colleagues do the same, I wonder whether we too, like dormant spores or viruses, ever exist in a state between living and dead – partially alive and partially dead. Scientists, doctors and ethicists have struggled with defining when life begins and ends. Does our life begin at conception, or when our embryonic heart begins to beat, or when we can survive outside our mother? Is a comatose individual declared dead when the heart stops beating or when the brain ceases electrical activity? When is it murder to take a comatose patient off life-support, and when is it kind, or practical, to do so? Do thoughts or feelings invade the comatose mind?

Don't ask Graham, a famous patient with a rare and weird medical condition – Cotard's syndrome – to answer these questions. Graham woke up one morning thinking he was dead. Yes, dead! But, of course, he wasn't. He woke up. Cotard's patients are certain that they are either dead or that parts of them are dead. Does this touch on being partially dead?

Poor Graham was seriously depressed. He said he destroyed his brain attempting suicide by taking a bath with an electrical device, and then he insisted that he was brain dead. According to psychologist Adam Zeman, Graham's condition was a "metaphor for how he felt about the world…his experiences no longer moved him…he felt he was in a limbo state caught between life and death." Graham lost his sense of smell and taste, he saw no point in eating or speaking or even thinking because he was dead, and nothing was meaningful to him anymore. He didn't even brush his teeth – why bother if he's dead? – and so they turned black. When Graham went to a local graveyard he wanted to stay there, the home of the dead, a place he felt at home. He imagined himself "walking dead."

Positron emission tomography (PET scans) showed abnormally low metabolic activity in Graham's frontal and parietal brain regions – the default mode network vital to consciousness that gives the ability to recollect the past or have a sense of self. Graham's PET scan resembled that of someone in a vegetative or anesthetized state. Although the cause remained mysterious, he did improve over time with therapy. He never felt completely normal, but he was able to live independently. Apparently, this form of "partial death" can be reversible to some extent, like that of dormant spores.

Graham's situation is a striking example of brain compartmentalization directing behavior and mental activity. Each individual is an integrated modular person. Our various movements, senses, thoughts, memories – traits defining us as living – have separate control centers in the brain. Are we partially "dead" when these master controls get scrambled or are selectively damaged and no longer function cohesively, as a machine that is broken when some of its parts fail to work properly?

A new form of partial death, or perhaps, more positively, partial life, or even potential life, was recently discovered. Cellular activity was restored in brains of slaughtered pigs. While still a far cry from awakening normal brain function or any kind of coordinated electrical signaling required for higher brain activity, some brain electrical activity was observed, blood vessels began to function and response to drugs was reactivated. Coupling these preliminary findings with routine organ transplants, including heart and lung transplants, raises, once again, the evasive question of how much of a living system must die before it is declared dead? Permanently dead, that is. Gone, completely, kaput.

We are complicated creatures bouncing between objective realities and subjective abstractions. Movement, replication, evolution, energy consumption, learning, reasoning, predicting – take your pick and add more – chess computers now defeat grand master chess players and artificial intelligence can design and interpret scientific experiments quicker and sometimes better (although they still lack judgment) than scientists. Many of the traits for living, as we define it, are shared with inanimate objects, leading to ambiguity of what's alive.

Frankenstein, Mary Shelley's innovative fantasy comes to mind about a creature ambiguously "alive." She dreamed up the story while on vacation in Switzerland with her husband, the poet Percy Shelley, and Lord Byron plus a few friends. (What a thrill it must have been to be a guest there!) How fitting that the first challenges to the concept of "living" arose with poets rather than scientists telling each other stories. *Frankenstein* is about a human-like monster – a misunderstood killer – made from exhumed spare parts of corpses. Shelley introduced ambiguity to the concept of "living" by having the title of the story *Frankenstein*, the creator (Dr. Victor Frankenstein) of the monster, not the monster. The monster remained nameless and referred to as the creature, fiend, daemon, and wretch at different times, leaving it in a suspended state – both alive and not alive. The book, published originally in 1818, gave birth to a fictional "person" assembled from dead organs, a feat of biological alchemy.

I am continually amazed how characters in literature – fiction that has nothing to do with real-life flesh – gain such traction, capture an emotional foothold and become alive for us. Stories, fiction, conceive "living" characters that outlive us. Falstaff, Sherlock Holmes, Lolita. The list is extensive. These names transform into suspended, immortal "life." These paper personalities fill a gap between real and unreal, alive and dead. "Life" congealed from air. How extraordinary is that!

The computer bestows "life" from machinery. The computer Hal, a pioneer computer "person," interacted with the spaceship crew in Stanley Kubrick's novel film, *The Space Odyssey*. Hal, an object, a machine, was "alive," as it were. Or, think of the lovable robots, R2D2 and C-3PO, made of steel and gears in *Star Wars*. They have human reactions and communicate with us – quite extraordinary. In the movie, *Her,* a lonely writer falls in love with the lovely human voice of an operating system who in virtual reality is a "living" machine. These constructions are both "dead" machines and "living" people. We accept robots as one of us to some extent and develop feelings for them: inanimate becomes animate in our minds. We wish them well, and we suffer if they're damaged or destroyed. We create suspended states of both "dead" and "alive."

In addition to perceiving a form of life in our minds from corpses or machines, there's also a case for "life" in the mere objects of art that stir our emotions and thoughts. The "voice" we hear is a blend of the artist's and our own – a dialogue between the messenger and ourselves. In my metaphorical short story, *Immobilon*, Syd, the paralyzed protagonist, is surrounded by his collection of Inuit art in his study and hears the sculptures speaking to him. Inuit sculptures also "speak" in a "language" that transcends words. My Inuit sculpture of a baby owl clinging to the back of its mother becomes art for me when I "feel" the mother's alert protectiveness and hear the baby say, "I love you, Mommy." It is then that I sense the power and meaning of this piece of art. Another example is Papa's emphasis on projecting feelings by playing the cello. He asked his students to say aloud, "I love you!" and "I hate you!" repeatedly until it was convincing. He wanted the music, the cello, to "speak" in a "language" that projected human emotion in order to transform notes into music and art. He wanted the cello, a box, to be "alive."

What's alive is what we make alive.

Acknowledgements

Many thanks to:

My instructors – especially Robert Bausch and Barbara Esstman – and colleagues in workshops at The Writer's Center in Bethesda;

Mia Garcia and Margaret Dimond for their invaluable help and advice in matters both big and small in my trek as a writer;

Adele Siegal for her eagle-eye proof reading;

Barbara Esstman and Lucy Chumbley for their encouragement and editing, improving the manuscript;

My publisher, Adelaide Books and Stevan Nikolic, for support and believing in me;

Ismael Carrillo for his excellent illustrations;

My wife Lona, for her painting of what appears as a "live" skeleton" atop a corpse, and as always, for her helpful comments and continual patience while my mind and moods wander from reality to fantasy and back again.

About the Author

During his 50-year career at the National Institutes of Health, Joram Piatigorsky has published some 300 scientific articles and a book, *Gene Sharing and Evolution* (Harvard University Press, 2007), lectured worldwide, received numerous research awards, including the prestigious Helen Keller Prize for vision research, served on scientific editorial boards, advisory boards and funding panels, and trained a generation of scientists. Presently an emeritus scientist, he collects Inuit art, and is Vice-Chairperson on the Board of Directors of The Writer's Center in Bethesda. He blogs (JoramP.com), has published personal essays in *Lived Experience* and *Adelaide Literary Magazine*, a novel, *Jellyfish Have Eyes* (IPBooks, 2014), a memoir, *The Speed of Dark* (AdelaideBooks, 2018) and a collection of short stories, *The Open Door and Other Tales of Love and Yearning* (AdelaideBooks, 2019). He has two sons, five grandchildren, and lives with his wife in Bethesda, Maryland. He can be contacted at joram@joramp.com.

www.ingramcontent.com/pod-product-compliance
Lightning Source LLC
Chambersburg PA
CBHW050441200726
48295CB00024B/897